For Trent

My dearest son,
just as you strengthen your muscles by using them,
you strengthen your heart by listening to it.
It makes me happy to know that Humphrey is there to help you.

I love you
Mom   C. N.

Copyright © 2000 by Nord-Süd Verlag AG, Gossau Zürich, Switzerland
First published in Switzerland under the title *Wer gewinnt?*

First published in the United States, Great Britain, Canada, Australia,
and New Zealand in 2000 by North-South Books,
an imprint of Nord-Süd Verlag AG, Gossau Zürich, Switzerland

Distributed in the United States by North-South Books Inc., New York.

Library of Congress Cataloging-in-Publication Data is available.
A CIP catalogue record for this book is available from The British Library.

ISBN 0-7358-1252-7 (trade binding)
1 3 5 7 9 TR 10 8 6 4 2
ISBN 0-7358-1253-5 (library binding)
1 3 5 7 9 LE 10 8 6 4 2

Printed in Belgium

For more information about our books, and the authors and artists
who create them, visit our web site: www.northsouth.com

CHARISE NEUGEBAUER

THE
REAL WINNER

ILLUSTRATED BY
BARBARA NASCIMBENI

A MICHAEL
NEUGEBAUER
BOOK

NORTH-SOUTH BOOKS
NEW YORK/LONDON

One day as Humphrey was going fishing,
he heard someone calling.
"Humphrey! Wait for me!" cried Rocky.
"Please, Humphrey, may I go with you?
Nobody wants to play with me."
Humphrey wasn't surprised. Rocky turned everything
into a contest, and if he didn't win,
he whined and cried. But Humphrey didn't mind.
He loved everyone, and everyone loved him.
So Humphrey agreed to let Rocky come fishing with him.
"Race you to the bridge, Humphrey! Race you!"
Humphrey ran as fast as he could.
As he passed Rocky,
Rocky whined, "That's not fair!"

Suddenly, Humphrey heard someone crying.
He stopped and looked around.
There was a little bird
that had fallen out of its nest.
Gently, Humphrey lifted the bird and
placed it safely back in its home.
Humphrey smiled and said, "Sing, little bird, sing."
And the little bird sang happily.
Only then did Humphrey remember the race,
but it was too late.
Rocky was on the bridge shouting,
"I won! I won! Wait 'til I tell my mom!"

As they crossed the bridge,
Rocky saw the stream.
"I bet I can beat you across!" Rocky shouted.
"Last one to the other side is a rotten egg!"
They jumped in and started swimming.
As Humphrey passed Rocky,
Rocky whined, "That's not fair!"
Suddenly, Humphrey heard someone crying.
He stopped and looked around.
There was a little duck
who couldn't find his family.

Gently, Humphrey guided the little duck around the rocks.
Humphrey smiled and said: "Swim, little duck, swim."
And the little duck swam happily back to his family.
Only then did Humphrey remember the race, but it was too late.
Rocky was on the other side of the stream shouting,
"I won! I won! Wait 'til I tell my mom!"

When they reached the fishing pond Rocky shouted,
"I bet I can catch the first fish, Humphrey! First fish wins!"
Rocky ran to the edge of the pond and started to fish.
Humphrey carefully baited his hook, and soon he felt a tug at his line.
"I think I've got one!" Humphrey shouted.
Rocky scowled. "That's not fair!" he whined.

Just then, Humphrey heard someone crying.
He looked around. There was a little frog
trapped inside a bucket.

Humphrey pulled his fishing line out of the water and carefully
lifted the frog out of the bucket. He smiled and said, "Jump, little frog, jump."
And the little frog happily jumped off across the grass.
Only then did Humphrey remember the contest, but it was too late.
Rocky was waving his fishing pole in the air, shouting,
"I won! I won!"
"Look again," said Humphrey.
"Old shoes don't count!"

"What?" said Rocky, puzzled.
When he saw what had happened,
he stopped smiling. "At least you're cleaning
up the pond," said Humphrey with a chuckle.
"Who cares," grumbled Rocky.
"I just want to catch a fish."

Humphrey helped Rocky remove the shoe. Rocky baited his hook again.
"Let's do some *real* fishing!" Rocky challenged.
"We'll take the boat. Then I *know* I'll catch a fish!"
They climbed into the boat and paddled out into the middle of the pond.
When they found a good spot, they started to fish again.

Humphrey watched how his line moved in the water.
He listened as the fish splashed and played.
He was enjoying himself so much that he forgot all about the contest.
But with every fish Rocky saw jumping and playing near the boat,
he looked more and more unhappy.

"It will be getting dark soon," said Humphrey.
He jumped into the water and swam to shore.
When Humphrey had gathered their things together,
he called to Rocky, "Time to go!"
Rocky panicked. "No, no! Not yet!" he cried.
"I need to catch a fish–just one!"
"Rocky," said Humphrey calmly,
"we've been here all afternoon.
The fish just aren't biting today."
Rocky didn't listen.
All he could think about was catching a fish
and winning the contest.
Humphrey wasn't surprised.
"Okay, Rocky," he said.
"Come back to shore. I'll try to help you."

Humphrey explained to Rocky that if he wanted to win, he had
to stop thinking about winning, and start thinking about the fish.
"Fish aren't in a hurry," he said. "So you can't fish fast."
"You have to relax and try to enjoy what you're doing."
Rocky tried to think about the fish,
but it was hard to stop thinking about winning.
"Close your eyes," whispered Humphrey. "Relax. Listen."
Rocky closed his eyes.

He thought about a fish with shiny scales.
He imagined it swimming zigzag through the water.
Rocky began to relax a little.
Then he felt a slight tug at his line. What if it's another shoe?
thought Rocky. Or a tin can? Then Rocky felt another tug.
He just knew it was a fish!
It didn't feel like a big fish, but that didn't matter.
If he got it to shore he would win!
"Slowly," said Humphrey, guiding Rocky.
Rocky concentrated.
"Think about the fish," he repeated to himself.
And suddenly, there it was!

Humphrey took the fish off the hook and handed it to Rocky.
"Congratulations, Rocky. You caught the first fish. You win."
Rocky looked at the winning fish. The poor little fish fought to free itself.
Humphrey looked at Rocky, puzzled. Rocky should be shouting,
"I won! I won! Wait 'til I tell my mom!"
But, he wasn't. He was just standing there.
Rocky didn't understand either. Why wasn't he happy?
He had won.

Rocky thought about the little fish
squirming to free itself from his grasp.
He thought about the little bird,
· the little duck, and the little frog.
Humphrey had been their friend.
Rocky looked at the little fish moving in his hands.
It was the winning fish.

Finally, Rocky smiled.
"Humphrey," he announced.
"Don´t you know, winning isn't everything!"
Then he shouted happily,
"Grow little fish, grow!" and he gently tossed the little fish
back into the pond.

That night when Rocky got home he told his family about the winning fish. His mother gave him a big kiss. "I've never been more proud of you!" she said.